"A warmly satisfying story. From the opening scene in the school cafeteria, complete with lunch bag auction and flying celery, children will feel right at home. Ben Shecter's amusing drawings echo the story's mood."—*Kirkus Reviews*

"As Thad explains it, it is easy to see why he and Maggie are mortal enemies: they can't keep from taunting each other. This amiable story is told and illustrated with humor, the characters come alive, and the classroom scenes are delightful."—*Bulletin of the Center for Children's Books*

"*Getting Something on Maggie Marmelstein* is funny, and boys and girls will recognize each other."—Los Angeles *Times*

"Genuine character and plot development with amusing dialog. The result: a book of general appeal that should prove enduring."—*Publishers Weekly*

Marjorie Weinman Sharmat

GETTING
SOMETHING
ON
MAGGIE MARMELSTEIN

Pictures by Ben Shecter

A Harper Trophy Book

HARPER & ROW, PUBLISHERS

*The author's father, Mr. Nathan Weinman, of Port-
land, Maine, has graciously consented to the use of
his bread pudding recipe on pp. 99–100 of this book.*

GETTING SOMETHING ON MAGGIE MARMELSTEIN

Text copyright © 1971 by Marjorie Weinman Sharmat

Illustrations copyright © 1971 by Ben Shecter

ISBN 0–06–440038–7

FOR MY SON ANDREW

Contents

GETTING SOMETHING ON
MAGGIE MARMELSTEIN

Meet Mouse
Maggie Marmelstein

My mother told me that I should never hate anybody, so I guess that I only dislike Maggie Marmelstein very very very very very much. Add a couple of "verys" to that, and you'll know how she feels about me. Maggie lives two doors away from me in an apartment house, and she is in my class at school. Sometimes I get to thinking how great it would have been if we had been born in different centuries. Or we could at least have lived on different continents, let alone the same apartment house. She could have been someone like Lucrezia Borgia over in Italy and I could have been someone like Daniel Boone in this country. We would have missed each other completely. Actually I would settle for Maggie just moving to the next block.

I suppose the main reason Maggie doesn't like me is because I once called her a mouse in front of a few kids. It is certainly not my fault that she squeaks like a mouse. It is only my fault that I mentioned it. To her. In front of people.

It happened in the lunchroom at school a couple of weeks ago. I walked in with my best friend, Henry, and a salami sandwich. Henry and I looked around for a place to sit. The lunchroom is always crowded and noisy. Some of the kids eat their lunch there, some of the kids throw their lunch there, and some do a little of each. Since Henry and I are both law-abiding, we had come only to eat.

There were some empty seats at a table with three kids from our class: Ellen, Noah, and Ronald the Rock Thrower. Ellen is a girl who never seems to take up as much space as she's entitled to, and she doesn't say much either. If the lunchroom were full of Ellens, everybody could hear everybody else chew. Noah is the boy version of Ellen, but it works out worse for Noah. Ellen is called shy, but Noah is called sissy. All the kids call Ronald the Rock Thrower Ronald the Rock Thrower. Like Billy the Kid or something. He always says much too much, and none of it is worth hearing.

Henry and I sat down. I had to sit beside Ronald, but I left a nice, roomy space between us. There was also a large-sized space between Ronald and Noah, who sat on Ronald's other side. In addition to his specialty, Ronald is an elbow pusher and occasional lunch snatcher.

I started to eat my salami sandwich. Enter Maggie Marmelstein who sat down beside Henry as I was enjoying my second bite. I was not happy to see her. Maggie has a miserable disposition and dark circles under her eyes which come from staying up nights watching The Late Show with her mother. I predict that the day her television set breaks down she will become a better person. She looked straight at me, as if Henry, who was between us, was transparent.

Maggie said, "Sandwiches should be seen and not smelled." She gave me her I-disapprove-of-salami-sandwiches look. Then she unwrapped her own sandwich.

"Whatcha got there?" asked Henry.

"This is an imported jam sandwich," said Maggie.

"Is the whole sandwich imported, or just the jam?" asked Henry.

"The jam is imported from England," said Maggie. "The bread comes from Hackensack, New Jersey."

"How do you know a thing like that?" asked Henry. "I don't know where my bread comes from."

"I read the bread wrapper," said Maggie.

"You read bread wrappers," I said. I started to laugh. "Are they interesting? I mean, is there a good plot, and how about the characters? Come on, tell us."

Maggie took a bite out of her Hackensack, New Jersey, bread. She was ignoring me.

That might have been the end of that if Noah hadn't spoken up. "I imagine that it could be very rewarding to read bread wrappers," he said. "For example, if you think of pieces of bread as the covers of a book, the ingredients on the wrapper actually tell you what is going on inside the covers."

I knew that Noah knew what he meant. But I didn't. What he said always came out too fancy, and he couldn't help it. Maybe that's why he didn't say much. But once in a while he would pipe up with something, as if he were practicing being brave and wanted to be prepared if a main bout came along. He had just knighted himself Maggie's Champion.

"Shut up, Noah," said Ronald the Rock Thrower.

"Ronald, you be quiet and stop picking on Noah," said Maggie who was now Noah's Champion. Maggie meant well, but now Noah had a girl protecting him. Noah's sissy title was not only intact, it was practically ablaze in neon lights.

A piece of celery from another table sailed through the air and landed on our table. Ronald threw it back.

"Can I have a bite of your salami sandwich?" Henry asked me.

"Sure," I said. "Hackensack, New Jersey, bread is funny looking anyway."

"I heard that," said Maggie. "But I'll ignore it."

"Thank you, wrapper reader," I said.

"I won't ignore *that*," said Maggie. "Calling me names. You're fresh."

"Like Hackensack, New Jersey, bread?" asked Henry. "Or like this?" He pinched Maggie on the arm.

It was just a quick little pinch, but Maggie squeaked, "Stop that, you."

"My friend is not a *you*," I said. "But you're a mouse. You squeak just like a mouse."

"Hey, everybody, meet Mouse Maggie Marmelstein," said Ronald.

"You," said Maggie to me, "are not a you. You are a rat."

If Maggie were a more original person she wouldn't have called me a rat after I called her a mouse. And if she were a more accurate person she wouldn't have called me a rat. If you could see me, you would realize at once that I bear no resemblance whatsoever to a rat.

Unfortunately Maggie didn't stop at calling me a rat. She then said, "You're a rat, Thaddeus Gideon Smith."

Thaddeus Gideon Smith the Fifth is my name but I keep it quiet. Sometimes in private Henry calls me Smith the Fifth, but everybody else calls me Thad. I was named after my father who was named after *his* father who was named after *his* father who was named after *his* father who did something important in the Civil War. Actually I like to say Thaddeus Gideon Smith to myself. My first ancestor who thought up the name probably went to plenty of bother to do it, and it shows. But when I grow up I'm changing my name to John Doe, which will be easy to write on my checks and my driver's license.

Henry and I left the table shortly after I was called a rat, Thaddeus Gideon Smith.

"Maggie's a pill," said Henry. "Calling her a

mouse is an insult to every living, breathing mouse."

"So she's a pill," I said. "So what? So I said she squeaked like a mouse. So what? So she called me a rat. I forgive her for calling me a rat. I forgive myself for saying she squeaks like a mouse. And I also forgive you and me for starting the fight."

Actually I wanted to make up with Maggie so she wouldn't go around calling me Thaddeus Gideon Smith.

How Can a Mouse Be a Princess?

Our first class after lunch is English. If there is any place wilder than our lunchroom, it is our English classroom. Our English class is taught by Miss Cecily Stemmish. Miss Stemmish is a sweet lady. She could never say no. She is the kind of teacher most kids temporarily want for their mother, because she would let them get away with murder. Long-term it would be a very bad deal in my opinion.

Our English class was putting on a one-act play for parents, based on the fairy tale of the princess and the frog. Originally our play was supposed to be about some spacemen and women who go to the moon and spend some time there and come back, and have some adventures going, spending, and coming. But we found out that another class was putting on a space play.

None of the kids wanted to do a fairy tale, and of

course they could have easily talked Miss Stemmish out of it. But the principal was another matter. He knew Miss Stemmish's weakness. I heard him tell her, "A fairy tale and that's it. The one about the princess and the frog. I always liked that one. See what you can do with it, Miss Stemmish."

Miss Stemmish had explained the story to us, although we already knew the plot. It's about this princess who makes friends with a frog who likes to talk a lot. She becomes convinced that the frog is really a prince who has been changed into a frog under the spell of an evil witch. She thinks that if the frog performs some noble deed—she isn't sure just what—the spell will be broken and he will be changed back into a prince and they will live happily ever after. So one day while she is chatting with him down by the pond where he lives, she accidentally hurts herself on a rock and starts to bleed. The frog rushes out of the water, gets help, and her life is saved and she kisses him and he turns into a prince on the spot.

"That's kid stuff," said Ronald the Rock Thrower.

Maybe he felt uncomfortable having a rock as co-villain with the witch.

"Perhaps we could vary the story just a bit if it

would make all of you happy," said Miss Stemmish.

"Yah," said Ronald and a few other kids. So we all talked it over. Miss Stemmish waited patiently. At last, Ronald, who had made himself the spokesman for the class, said, "A frog is a frog, let's face it. You can stand on your head or roll somersaults, and you still can't change a frog into a prince. So in this play he stays a frog, and a real prince comes along to marry the princess after she recovers."

Miss Stemmish sighed. "I hope the principal likes it. He's so accustomed to it the other way."

I had a crazy urge to walk right up to Miss Stemmish and pat her hand and say, "There, there. It's going to be all right, Miss Stemmish." But I knew I couldn't do it. She might be extremely grateful and kiss me.

Miss Stemmish was trying to gather up courage. Suddenly her head and arms rose together as if jerked up by an invisible amateur puppeteer. She was, she thought, *in command*.

"First, class, we will audition for the princess role," she said.

"I want it. It's mine!" yelled Ronald.

Miss Stemmish's head and arms sagged. The puppeteer must have dropped the strings and quit.

Ronald was too much for most of the teachers, but he shook up Miss Stemmish the most. He will probably grow up to be what is known as a pillar of society because he has no place to go but up. Grownups will root for Ronald every inch of the way, and everyone will rush to shake his hand when he lands up in college instead of Sing Sing.

Maggie said, "I would like to audition for the princess role. May I start now?"

Maggie sounded sincere and earnest, and everybody turned toward her. "How could a mouse play a princess," I said to Henry. Maggie gave me a dirty look.

Miss Stemmish perked up. "You may begin, Maggie," she said. "Oh, wait. The play is very rough and unpolished at present, and it also is about to undergo drastic surgery. So would you like to audition with lines from another play?"

"Well, as it happens," squeaked Maggie, "I've written a little script myself about Queen Elizabeth the First."

"Oh my goodness," said Miss Stemmish. "Aren't you resourceful."

Maggie walked to the front of the room. "I am Queen Elizabeth the First of England," she said, dropping her squeak for the occasion. "*I* am the Queen."

Henry whispered to me, "I thought she was trying out for princess. Already she's got herself a promotion."

This speech was probably the result of Maggie's watching The Late Show and the news in the same night.

All of a sudden, Ronald yelled, "I'll vote for you anytime, Maggie."

Noah looked angry, as if he wanted to clout Ronald. Come on, Noah, I thought. You can do it. You can do it. You can break the sissy spell. Sock him.

But Noah only said something in a low voice.

Fortunately Miss Stemmish said more. She sent Ronald to the principal's office. It was a surprise move. It was a good move.

Then Miss Stemmish said, "That was excellent, excellent, Maggie. Now who else would like to audition for the princess part?"

Maggie hadn't finished her Queen Elizabeth speech. She waited for someone to remind Miss Stemmish.

Nobody spoke up. Except me. "Maggie Marmel-

stein is still trying out," I said. Why did I say it?

Miss Stemmish apologized to Maggie. Maggie turned right back into Queen Elizabeth the First and went on with her speech. She didn't look my way. I didn't expect her to say thank you to me then and there, because queens often ignore favors from commoners. Her speech was convincing. It seemed to me that Maggie could have talked herself into becoming Queen of England. There was something strong about her, and scary, too.

After Maggie was through, Miss Stemmish called for more girls to try out for the princess role. But nobody dared after Maggie's performance.

"Well, then," said Miss Stemmish, "Maggie Marmelstein is our princess."

Maggie gave a little squeak. Royalty hadn't changed her.

Who Would Like To
Try Out for Frog?

"Who would like to try out for Frog?" asked Miss Stemmish.

Heads turned throughout the room to see who would raise his hand. But the only movement was head-turning.

"We are now accepting auditions for the frog role," said Miss Stemmish in a slightly louder voice.

More head-turning. Nobody wanted to try out. It didn't matter whether the frog stayed a frog or not, nobody wanted to be him. So Miss Stemmish said, "We'll go on to the other roles, and get back to the frog part later. I really do think that it's an extremely challenging role. The frog is articulate, well-bred, and a credit to all amphibians."

That description did a good job of changing the mind of any kid who had been weakening and thinking about playing the frog. A plain frog might be hard to cast, but a stuffed-shirt frog was practically an impossibility.

Miss Stemmish went on. "Not all of us are destined to be stars, but we can still shine in lesser roles. Who of you, who honestly believe you are not of star caliber, would like to play the palace people?"

Every hand in the class shot up except Maggie's. Here was everybody's chance to make sure they were eliminated from the frog part.

"You can't all be that," said Miss Stemmish. "I still need a king, a queen, a palace physician, and a prince."

Maggie raised her hand. "Ellen would make a beautiful queen, and Noah would make a real smart doctor."

Ellen who was suddenly officially beautiful and Noah who was suddenly officially smart smiled at each other. They were too terrified to do anything else. That included being too terrified to turn down the queen and doctor roles even if they wanted to. Maggie sure came on strong with her ideas.

At that moment Ronald walked in with the principal. He walked back to his seat while the principal talked to Miss Stemmish. The principal kept his voice low, but I heard him say something about "constructive instead of destructive." Then he left. Miss Stemmish faced the class and announced, "I have made a decision about the prince. Ronald will be the prince."

The kids in the class looked bewildered. Was the prince part some kind of punishment or some kind of reward? I believe that the principal and Miss Stemmish were trying to reform Ronald. But what terrible casting.

Miss Stemmish asked Ralph, the tallest boy in the class, to be the king, because he was "too regal to be just a palace person."

Regal Ralph, regal red faced Ralph, said okay.

The only role still up for grabs was the frog.

The bell rang. Class was over. I rushed up to Maggie. She would certainly want to be friends since I had saved her queen speech from being finished before it was finished.

"Congratulations, Princess," I said.

She said, "Thanks, Thaddeus Gideon Smith, you rat."

So Maggie went around spreading the word that my real name is Thaddeus Gideon Smith the Fifth. And she was a topnotch spreader. If Maggie had lived in the days of the Town Crier she would have been one. Except Maggie's cry would have been "All's terrible."

I gave Maggie the silent treatment whenever I saw her. It was the easiest form of retaliation. I didn't have to pick and choose among all the nasty names I could have called her. But don't get the idea that I was really bothered by Maggie. She developed this rotten little habit of saying, "Hello, Thaddeus Gideon Smith," every time she saw me, and it seemed to bring her a great deal of happiness.

Then trouble, real trouble, finally came. In the form of bread pudding.

Mrs. Marmelstein
Mixes Me Up

There are some things not worth getting into trouble over, and high on that list is bread pudding. This is how the bread pudding got into my life. I am one of those good kids who picks up his room without being asked and goes on errands he doesn't want to go on. So my mother was sure that I would go down the hall for her and borrow a cup of sugar from Maggie Marmelstein's mother. My mother could have gone herself, but she said that Maggie's mother talked so much the sugar would cost her three hours.

I said okay to my mother and went off, off to trouble with an empty measuring cup as my passport.

I rang the bell of 2B. Mrs. Marmelstein opened the door. She has fat arms and fat legs and a fat face and all together they make her look like she is full of love and good food.

She yawned. "Excuse me," she said. "I was up late watching television. A Clark Gable picture. Before he got his moustache." She looked at my measuring cup. "Flour or sugar?" she asked.

"Sugar," I said.

"Good. I'm overstocked. Can you come in and wait a minute? I'm in the middle of a pudding."

We went into her kitchen. It was a mess. On a quick count, there were twenty-two different boxes, jars, cans, and bottles. There were also some empty bread wrappers. I couldn't see whether Hackensack, New Jersey, was printed on them.

"You see all these things," said Mrs. Marmelstein. "Most of them went into this pudding. Here. Give it a taste and tell me if it's any good. Be honest now." She took a big dripping spoon from the mixing bowl and put it into my mouth.

"Mmmm," I said. Then she took some for herself with the same spoon.

I've noticed that the nicest people seem to be the least sanitary and some day I'm going to look into that situation. I was also wondering how a real nice lady like Mrs. Marmelstein could land up with an awful kid like Maggie.

"It's a bread pudding," said Mrs. Marmelstein. "It's a mixture of dark bread, white bread, eggs,

milk, raisins, dark sugar, white sugar, nuts, cinnamon . . ."

I interrupted Mrs. Marmelstein. From the looks of her kitchen, if she named everything, I might be there until midnight. "Where did you get the recipe?" I asked.

"Up here," she said, pointing to her head. "I cook by ear, like some people play the piano. Want another taste?"

She held out the spoon. I looked at it hard.

"You don't like the pudding?" she said. "Maybe it needs a little something more. Any ideas?"

I looked around. There was a banana on the counter. It was turning black and it didn't appear to have much of a future strictly as a banana. "How about a banana?" I said.

"A banana? Perfect," she said. "It will give the pudding an interesting texture." She took the banana from the counter and mashed it into the bowl.

Mrs. Marmelstein was so pleased with my suggestion that I looked around for more ideas. There were some jars of jelly that she had probably forgotten to put away after breakfast. "Grape jelly and apricot jelly will give it a terrific fruit flavor," I said.

"Why not?" said Mrs. Marmelstein, and she dumped large hunks of each into the bowl. "You've got the makings of a good cook," she said.

I didn't want to be a good cook. It is a great thing to be if you are grown-up. If you're a woman, you can have fifteen chins hanging down and a stomach out to *there* and people will praise you and say, "She's a wonderful cook, you can tell by looking at her." Or you can be a man and have a French accent and a white uniform and a job in a fancy restaurant and people might say, "He's a culinary genius." But if you're a boy cook, if you're smart, you'll hide your cookbook inside a book jacket that says *Baseball Heroes of the 20th Century*.

Mrs. Marmelstein kept telling me what a good cook I was and she got me to stir her pudding around while she looked for new ingredients on the shelf. She also tied an apron around me without asking my permission, and since I am a real polite kid in addition to being a helpful one, I couldn't tell her that it made me feel like a complete dumb-dumb.

So I stood there, wrapped in Mrs. Marmelstein's apron and stirring with what seemed to be the only spoon she had to her name, when Maggie walked into the room.

"If You Tell on Me, I'll Tell on You."

I kept on stirring. There was a slight chance that this was all a dream and at any moment a huge iron claw would come down from the ceiling, scoop me up, and deposit me back in my apartment.

Maggie squeaked sweetly—and it *is* possible to do that—"Hello."

No Thaddeus Gideon Smith the Fifth. Just hello. I was suspicious. I was afraid that Maggie was dropping Thaddeus Gideon Smith because she could replace it with something much worse.

I said, "I've gotta go."

"You've been a real help to me," said Mrs. Marmelstein.

I wished she hadn't said that. In fact I wished she hadn't answered the door when I rang the bell. I wished she had still been watching Clark Gable without his moustache, and hadn't even thought about making bread pudding.

"Don't forget your sugar," she said, and she poured some into my measuring cup.

"Don't forget your sugar," squeaked Maggie, and she smiled a smile that she must have copied from Count Dracula on The Late Show.

I took off the apron. I felt like draping it over Maggie's shoulders—a cape for Countess Dracula Marmelstein.

I turned to go and Maggie squeak-whispered to me, "I'm going to tell every kid in this building and every kid on this block and every kid in school and maybe every kid in the world that you're a sissy cook." Then she ran off.

I walked back to my apartment with the cup of sugar. I was worried. Maggie definitely would tell all the kids that I was doing girl's work. And they *would* think I was a *sissy*.

There are not too many ways to stop a girl. I couldn't even consider giving Maggie a bloody nose. I could call her a name like tomboy. But a girl doesn't mind being called a tomboy as much as a boy minds being called a sissy.

I decided I'd tell Maggie that if she told on me, I'd tell something on her. So what did I know about

Maggie that she didn't want anybody else to know? Nothing. That's the trouble with people like Maggie. They can be horrible without breaking any rules. Maggie is always on time for school, she's prissy polite, saying thank you and please to the teachers, and she keeps her fingernails clean. Once in a while she even brings an apple to a teacher.

All of a sudden I knew that I knew how to stop Maggie. I got a pencil and paper and started to write. The words I wrote were beautiful:

IF YOU TELL ON ME I'LL TELL ON YOU
AND YOU KNOW WHAT

I underlined WHAT three more times.

I hoped that Maggie knew what WHAT was, because I didn't. All I knew was that everybody has something to hide, everybody has a WHAT in their lives.

I put the paper in an envelope and wrote MAGGIE across the front. Then I went back to Maggie's apartment and slipped the envelope under the door. I started to walk away. Then suddenly Mrs. Marmelstein opened the door. She looked surprised to see me, but she smiled. Her surprise smile was as nice as her regular one.

"Uh, is Maggie still home?" I asked. "I have a note for her—down there." I pointed to the floor, and I started to leave again.

"A note for my Maggie," she said. "How nice." Then she called, "Maggie, there's a note at the door for you."

I heard Maggie squeak and come running toward us. Come on, Maggie, I said to myself, come running for your cheese, and don't squeak too hard when the trap closes on you.

When Maggie saw me and the envelope she squeaked, "A note from YOU?" She stepped back.

I'll say this for Maggie she knew poisoned cheese when she smelled it.

Suddenly she grabbed the envelope and ran.

"Maggie forgot her manners," said Mrs. Marmelstein. "I'll call her back. We can all have some bread pudding together. It's almost through baking."

"Later, thank you," I said. Like fifty years later, I thought.

I went back to my apartment and called Henry to come over. It's hard to do something very clever and not share it. Henry was the best person to share it with. He thinks I'm terrific.

When he got to my apartment I told him about

my clever note to Maggie, and why I had to write it. I can trust Henry as much as I can trust myself.

"Just wait," I said. "She'll be at my door absolutely begging me not to tell."

The doorbell rang. Henry ran to the door. Then he called to me, "It's the beggar."

I walked to the door slowly. I enjoyed every step. There was Mouse Maggie. She opened her mouth. She squeaked one word, "TELL!" Then she walked away.

I must say that Henry did try very hard not to laugh.

"Now you're really in trouble," he said. "You're in a stew over bread pudding."

When Henry starts telling jokes I wish I were a million miles away.

"It's not funny," I said. "Maggie will spread that bread pudding story . . ."

"Like mustard on a hot dog," laughed Henry.

"Are you her friend or mine?" I asked.

"What kind of question is that?" said Henry. "I like Maggie as much as a homework assignment."

Henry didn't like Maggie because Maggie didn't like me. I liked that about Henry.

"Well then, what can I do about her?" I asked.

"What can WE do about her?"

"Nothing," said Henry. "She's probably already started to tell people anyway. They'll kid you for a few days, but after a while they'll forget."

Henry had a joke about forgetting that he was about to tell. But I stopped him. "Maggie never forgets," I said. "And she'll never forget that she's the winner and I'm the loser."

"So lose her," said Henry. "*Really* get something on her. Then you'll be the winner. Or at least it will be a tie."

Henry, my friend Henry, my great friend Henry was a smart kid. I congratulated myself on being smart enough to have a friend as smart as Henry. Thanks to Henry I had a new goal. And that goal was GETTING SOMETHING ON MOUSE MAGGIE MARMELSTEIN.

Ellen Helps Us
Get Nowhere

The next day I found out for myself what my mother has been telling me right along: it is easier to have a goal than to achieve it. It was the first day of my GSOMMM campaign. (Henry and I decided to give it initials, because that made it more official. We wished that the initials spelled out a definite word or at least something we could pronounce easily, but it could have been worse, like XQSTRV or LMZDFD.)

I met Henry at eight o'clock in the morning at our usual corner. We walk to school together every day, except if one of us is very late. But we were both on time Monday because we had planned it that way. At the corner we stood and waited. We were waiting for Ellen. Ellen is a very good friend of Maggie's, but they fight once in a while. I knew they had a fight a few days ago, and that they would probably make up at any moment. Their fights last from two to five days on average. So we had to speak to Ellen before the five days were up. If she had anything to spill about Maggie, she would spill it now.

Ellen didn't know that we were waiting for her. If she had known she would have been suspicious. We ignore Ellen most of the time because she is so easy to ignore.

Henry was kind of jumpy. "I don't like to wait for somebody who doesn't know we're waiting for her," he said. He bent down and tied his shoelace which he had just untied. As long as he kept busy, he didn't feel so much like a waiter who shouldn't be waiting. "What happens when Ellen shows up?" he asked.

"We'll all walk to school together," I said. "We'll walk and talk. She's our best chance of GSOMMM. Look, here she comes."

Ellen was coming down the street. She walks like she sits, as if she doesn't want to use up any more room than absolutely necessary.

"Hello, Ellen," I said.

"Hello," she said.

I smiled.

She smiled.

Henry and I started to walk beside her. I said, "I hear that you're mad at Maggie Marmelstein."

Ellen didn't say anything. Her silence was like an empty space, and it was up to me to fill it up.

I said, "I'm mad at Maggie, too. We could maybe be mad together. Why are you mad?"

"Why are you mad?"

"You first," I said. I don't know why I said that. Having lived practically her whole lifetime being second, Ellen wasn't going to change for me. So now there was more empty space.

Then Henry said to Ellen, "In your opinion, how could Maggie be a better, finer, nicer, greater person?"

"She could be better, finer, nicer, and greater if she minded her own business," said Ellen. "Especially about lunch. That's how we had our fight. Ronald the Rock Thrower has been stealing my lunches, so I've been having my mother pack different kinds. I'm hoping to find something he doesn't like that I like, so he won't bother me anymore. But he keeps on liking everything. Anyway, last week, after he took part of my lunch, Maggie yelled after him, 'Ellen says you're going to get into plenty of trouble if you take her lunch again. Ellen's father weighs 235 pounds.' Well, I never said any such thing. And I told Maggie I never said it. And she said, 'Somebody's got to put words in your mouth because you won't.' Then Maggie got mad, so I got mad."

"Maggie talks too much," I said. "Why, I bet she told you plenty of her secrets when you were friends."

The minute I said that sentence I didn't like myself as much as before I said it. I believe in secrets, even though they are more for girls than boys. Telling a secret is bad, but trying to get somebody else to spill a secret is practically a crime. So I was kind of relieved when Ellen didn't say anything.

I guess Henry was relieved, too. He changed the subject. "What did you bring for lunch today?" he asked.

"A cream cheese sandwich with pieces of sardines stuck in it," she said. "Say, do you think if I took stewed prunes spread on wheat germ bread that Ronald wouldn't bother me anymore? That's what Maggie takes. Her mother makes the prune spread. Maggie tells everybody it's imported jam and they believe it."

"Did you say stewed prunes spread on wheat germ bread?" asked Henry. "That rhymes."

"And that's pretty silly," I said. "No wonder Maggie doesn't want it known."

"I shouldn't have told," said Ellen. "Maggie will be mad at me."

"You forgot. She already is," I said. "But we're your friends, right, Henry?"

"Right-O," said Henry. Then he and I rushed ahead so we could talk alone. "If I were Ellen, I wouldn't want friends like us," said Henry. "*Stewed prunes spread on wheat germ bread.* That's funny, but it's not as bad as what Maggie's got on you. Too bad Ellen wouldn't tell us a bunch of those secrets. I bet they're lulus."

"I wouldn't tell if I were Ellen," I said. "I wouldn't tell a friend's secrets. And Maggie *is* her friend. Look how she went after Ronald the Rock Thrower for Ellen. That's a friend. I'd do that for you, Henry."

"And I'd do that for you," said Henry.

"I'm glad to hear you say that, Henry, because Ronald the Rock Thrower is next on my list. My GSOMMM list."

"Oh, no," said Henry. "Why him?"

"Because he definitely is not a friend of Maggie's."

"He also definitely is not a friend of ours," said Henry.

"But we see him at school anyway," I said. "After all, he is in our class. And he doesn't keep rocks in the classroom."

"You go talk to him," said Henry, "and let me know what happens."

And so I found out how far Henry's friendship with me went. It stopped short of Ronald's rock-throwing range.

We were almost at school. Henry slowed down and said, "On second thought, what Ellen told us is pretty good. I mean, it is something. The more I think about it, the more I think it's good enough."

I was disappointed in Henry. How could he be satisfied with a very minor victory? "Henry, you've got to aim high."

"That's what Ronald the Rock Thrower does," said Henry.

"Okay, we'll forget him," I said. "But we've really got to get something big on Maggie. If this stewed prunes news got around, she probably wouldn't even care. I want her to *squirm*."

"A small victory is better than no victory," said Henry.

"Yes, but a major victory is even better. And my major victory plan is forming this very minute," I said. "Why should I try to get information about Maggie from other people when I can get it myself. Firsthand. How's this? Maggie is the princess in the class play, and I'm going to get a certain part in it and I'm going to watch her every second of every minute of every hour we're rehearsing."

"But there's only one part left," said Henry.

"And that's the part I want," I said. "It's the part opposite Maggie."

"The frog? You'd be the frog?" asked Henry.

"Hello, Frog.
Are You New Here?"

I went straight up to Miss Stemmish, even though my English class was later in the day. I said, "Meet your new frog."

"Why, you're positively *brave*," said Miss Stemmish. "You're a brave, dear, sweet boy. You'll make a magnificent frog."

I knew she meant that as a compliment. I was brave to take on the part that nobody wanted, and everybody would know I was brave for doing it. If I had immediately said I would be the frog, they might have laughed. But now I was daring to do something no one else had dared to do. Only Henry and I knew the real reason I'd become such a good sport.

Nothing, absolutely nothing, happened during class time or at recess or during lunch. By nothing

I mean that nobody came up and called me a cook. And Maggie simply acted as if I'd ceased to exist. I knew that somewhere there was an ax with my name and address on it, and it was scheduled to fall on me, but I did not know when or where.

Miss Stemmish waited until after school to tell our English class that they were no longer frogless. We were all assembled in the auditorium for rehearsal.

"Class, class," she said. "I have splendid news. We now have a frog. Thad is our frog."

I heard laughter. How could they laugh? Those cowards, slinking around as palace people. They were laughing at me because I was brave. They were laughing to cover their jealousy, those petrified palace people. Well, some of the great men of history have been laughed at.

There were a few non-laughers. Henry, of course, Ellen, Noah—and Maggie. Maggie squeaked, "Oh." For a moment I thought she might drop out of the princess part, but she didn't. She looked at me and I didn't like the look, so I gave her the same kind of look back. She said, "So *Thaddeus Gideon Smith the Fifth* is our frog." But she didn't laugh.

She was back to her old name-calling, and I was

afraid she was going to say more. But Miss Stemmish spoke up. "Here are your lines," she said to me. "Please have them completely memorized by the end of this week. Don't forget, we have only eleven days left until opening night." (Opening night and closing night were the same night, but Miss Stemmish believed in thinking positive.)

I already knew some of the frog lines, because the whole class had gotten together to write them and to fix up some of the other dialogue. Miss Stemmish hadn't told the principal about the class rewriting the play, including that the frog stayed a frog. "We'll surprise him," she said.

"Princess, you come on first," she said. "Walk up to the pond and sit down. Frog, you should already be in the pond. The green rug in the middle of the stage. Fortunately for us, I found it in my attic. I thought I had given it to the Salvation Army."

Maggie loved being called Princess. I wasn't so wild about my frog name.

"You may commence," said Miss Stemmish.

Maggie said, "Hello, Frog. Are you new here? I never noticed you in the pond before."

I said, "Hello, Princess. This is my first day in the pond."

"Where do you come from, O Frog?"

"From a land far away, O Princess. I hitched a ride on the back of an unwary stranger."

"I don't believe your story, O Frog. I think that you arrived magically. I think that you are really a prince and that a wicked witch cast a spell over you. That's what I think."

"You're entitled," I said. "But you've read too many stories. I am just a plain frog. There's nothing special about me."

"You said it," said Maggie.

"Wait!" called Miss Stemmish. "That's not the correct line, Maggie. The correct line is 'You seem very special to me'."

"I'm *terribly* sorry," said Maggie.

Maggie was not *terribly* sorry, or any other kind of sorry.

Miss Stemmish said, "Sit closer to the pond now, Maggie. You're getting more and more interested in the frog."

Maggie moved onto my green rug. If it had been a real pond, she'd have been soaked. She whispered to me, "I'm just waiting for the right moment to tell everybody about you, O Cook. I want a big audience."

I had a feeling of real terror. I was up against Mastermouth Marmelstein.

Suddenly I wanted the old green rug to be a magic carpet. I wanted to step off of it and, with Maggie still on it, command it to take off instantly for the other side of the world and remain there forever.

But all I could do was whisper back to Maggie, "If you dare to say it during the play, everyone will think you goofed a line. Nobody will believe it's real."

"Yes, they will," said Maggie. "And what's more, I'm not telling you when, where, or how I'll do it. Oh, by the way, I think you make a perfect frog."

"Well, as I mentioned to you before, you make a perfect mouse."

Miss Stemmish called, "Princess! Frog! I'm glad that you have so much to say to each other. But please do save all those lovely words until after rehearsal. Let's continue now."

Princess Maggie continued. "You seem very

special to me," she said. "If you tell me what kind of spell was cast over you, I'll try to get rid of it for you."

"No spell, O Princess. I was born a frog and I'll die a frog and I cannot be a prince in between."

"Very well, O Frog. I'll have to guess what the spell is, because I still believe there is one. But for now, I will say good-bye. My parents back at the palace will miss me. See you tomorrow."

"Same time, same station, O Princess."

"Wait!" cried Miss Stemmish. "That last line must go. It's an anachronism. If you don't know what that is, please look it up as part of tomorrow's assignment. I must tell you, Princess and Frog, that your language is not, well, poetic, at all. We should rewrite this scene."

"I've got it all memorized," squeaked Maggie. I noticed that her squeak had completely disappeared while she was the princess.

"I haven't," I said. "And if it makes Miss Stemmish happy, and if it improves the play, I'm all for having the scene rewritten."

"Spendid," said Miss Stemmish. "I will reinstate some of my original lines, and I will prepare some new ones. I'm sorry, Maggie."

I smiled. It wasn't even a minor victory, it was smaller than minor—but it was nice. I didn't give Maggie a chance to say anything. I hopped off the stage. I had to practice my hop, anyway.

Henry Saves Me

Walking home from school, Henry asked, "Well did you find out anything while you were a frog?"

"Nothing yet, but this is just the first day. I have plenty of time. She did tell me that she hasn't spread the cook story yet. She's waiting for the right moment and she wants an audience."

"She's sure dramatic, isn't she?" said Henry.

"Among other things," I said.

I felt a light tap on my arm. I turned around. It was Ellen.

"Thad," she said, "I think you are a real good actor, and also the kids weren't nice to laugh at you, but they weren't making fun of you because there is something about anybody, any human being being a frog, that might make people laugh about it and not mean it in a mean way."

Ellen had rehearsed that speech just for me. I

could tell. She said it the way she said her queen lines. Like she was hypnotized. But she said it. Ellen could talk if she forgot about herself. Maybe if Queen Ellen did very well in the play, just plain Ellen would think more of herself. Maybe Maggie Marmelstein thought so, too, when she got Ellen the part. I noticed that Maggie spent more time at rehearsals helping Ellen be a queenly queen than she did reading over her own lines. And I knew that Ellen and Maggie were really friends again because Ellen had a line today which went "Oh, Daughter, I've missed you" and she said *that* line with feeling.

Ellen walked on.

Henry said, "That was nice of Ellen to tell you what she told you. But how come she came up and said it? I mean *first* and all."

"I don't know," I said. "But I think it's a good sign."

The next day Miss Stemmish said, "I suggest that the main characters in the play spend some time together in an informal way so that they can exchange ideas and chat about their roles and possibly improve upon them."

So at lunch, the king, queen, princess, frog, palace physician, prince, and some of the palace people, including Henry, sat together. On this particular day we were holding an auction. Whenever someone is dissatisfied with the lunch his mother packed him (and this is often) there is an auction, and the lunch goes to the highest bidder. Henry was very unhappy about the cucumber sandwich and vegetable drink his mother had given him. She had said to him, "Vitamins, not junk, Henry. That's what I packed for you." Henry knew then that it would be ghastly. He wanted to auction it off for junk.

"I have here," he said, holding up his closed lunch bag, "a nutritious, delicious parcel. What'll you give me for it?"

"One broken potato chip," said Ronald. Ronald always started off the bidding. Nobody paid any attention to him.

"Five carrot sticks, washed and peeled," said Ralph the king.

"I hear five carrot sticks, washed and peeled," said Henry. "Who will bid more?"

"An unopened 1⅛ ounce bag of Cheez Doodles," said a palace person.

"The carrot sticks and three giant pretzels, salted," said Ralph.

"My whole lunch," said Ellen. "If you really don't like yours, I'll swap."

"No sacrifices," said Henry.

Ellen looked down.

"Come to think of it," said Henry, "you just gave me a legitimate bid and it was the highest legitimate bid. Going, going, gone to the highest bidder." He handed his lunch bag to Ellen, and she handed hers to him.

I am proud to have Henry for my best friend. I knew that he knew that Ellen's mother packs kookier sandwiches and kookier drinks than his mother. She does this to keep Ronald the Rock Thrower permanently discouraged from trying to take Ellen's lunch. But Henry did not want to turn Ellen down.

Ellen opened Henry's ex-bag. Ellen will eat anything, absolutely anything. "A cucumber sandwich," she said in a soft just-what-I-always-wanted voice.

"And see what I've got," said Henry in a loud just-what-I-always-wanted voice. He was waiting for someone to identify it because he couldn't. "And it tastes great." He said the last sentence before he bit into the sandwich, but I think I was the only one who noticed. Henry is a gentleman.

Maggie squeaked up. "It's fun to talk about food, isn't it. How many of you here have ever had bread pudding?"

I dropped my sandwich. Henry dropped his. Now I knew what best friendship was: loyalty and reflex action.

Henry picked up his sandwich and said, "Let's talk about the play. I think the palace should be painted blue. A medium shade of blue. Not too light, not too dark."

Maggie said, "How many of you here have ever *made* bread pudding?"

Henry said, "Miss Stemmish is calling you, Thad. I can hear her. She wants you IMEEEEEEEDI-ATELY."

"I didn't hear anybody call," said Noah, who thought he had just entered a safe conversation. "But Miss Stemmish has a high voice. Perhaps you have, in common with dogs and dolphins, the fact that you can hear at a range above normal human hearing."

"Exactly," said Henry. "SO SCRAM, THAD."

"Although," said Noah, "on reflection, the human

voice could not go that high. So that couldn't have been Miss Stemmish's voice. . . ."

I was already leaving the lunchroom, and I kept on going.

Later on, just before English class, I thanked Henry and asked him if Maggie had said anything more after I left.

"No, she was quiet as a—*you know what*. But I do have some news. You'll never guess who's doing your costume for the play. One guess."

"Mrs. Marmelstein," I said.

"How did you know?" asked Henry.

"She sews while she watches television. She could outfit an army."

"She's not doing the whole cast," said Henry. "They've got some stuff left over from other years. She's just doing the palace physician, the frog, and the princess, of course. You have to go over to her place for a fitting."

"Never! It'll be bread pudding all over again. How come she doesn't do it at school?"

"Look, she's doing the school a favor," said Henry. "Anyway, you can go over when Maggie isn't there. She'll be rehearsing with the palace people after school this Thursday. The frog isn't needed. Anyway, don't you think the apartment might be a good place for GSOMMM?"

"Not until this very minute," I said. "Thanks, pal."

"I've Got a Little Treat for the Cast."

After school I went back on the green rug, with Maggie dangling her foot over it. We were going to do the scene where she cuts her hand and I hop for help. We were waiting for King Ralph and Queen Ellen to finish their scene.

This was my second rehearsal with Maggie. The play was getting somewhere, but I was getting nowhere in GSOMMM. I watched Maggie all the time. I listened. I was always on duty. But what good had it done me? I noticed that she had a mole on her neck that I hadn't noticed before. Big deal. She whispered with Ellen and some of the other girls, but I could never hear what they were whispering about. It wasn't fair. Maggie only had to walk into her mother's kitchen to get something on me, but I had to turn myself into a frog, and I still landed up with nothing. Being a frog wasn't as bad as I had thought it would be, and I think Maggie was surprised that I played the role so well. But my inner, secret role was a flop. I felt like a loser. A cook, and now a loser, Thaddeus Gideon Smith the Fifth was only a success at being a frog.

"All right, Princess and Frog, you're on," called Miss Stemmish.

Maggie held her hand high. "Oh, oh," she said. "I have cut my hand on a rock. And it hurts."

"I will go to the palace for help," I said. "I will hop as fast as I can. Do not go away, O Princess."

"I cannot," said Maggie. "I am bleeding too hard, O Frog."

I hopped over to the side of the stage where the palace was.

"Is there a doctor in the house?" I asked.

"No, no, no," called Miss Stemmish. "You say, is the palace physician here."

"Is the palace physician here?" I asked.

"I am here," said Noah the palace physician.

Noah had gotten to like the part. I noticed that he was getting ever so slightly bolder, and he actually wrote himself some extra lines.

I think the main reason Noah liked being the doctor was because it gave him a chance to carry a big black bag, which he could use as a weapon if Ronald decided to attack him.

"Come quickly," I said to Doc Noah. "The princess is hurt."

Noah came quickly. Then we were both back at the green rug, where Maggie was lying with her hand in some ketchup. Miss Stemmish had wanted to wait until dress rehearsal to use the ketchup, but Maggie said she wouldn't be able to act bloody without it.

"I will bind up your wound," said Noah. "And you will be all right." (Originally we had written that he should also give the princess two aspirin, but Miss Stemmish had said, "No, no, a thousand times, no!")

Noah went on. "This frog here has saved your life."

"That's it!" cried Maggie, who was quite peppy considering that she had been bleeding to death minutes before. "That is just how a frog could lift the evil spell. I will kiss you, O Frog, and you will become a prince."

Maggie leaned over and gave me the shortest kiss on record. Her mouth was leaving my cheek almost before it arrived. The kiss tickled like a buttercup, and I wanted to scratch the place but I didn't dare.

Actually the kiss wasn't too bad, but also it wasn't too good. The kids laughed in a silly way, as if they had been kissed, too.

Then Maggie said, "Why aren't you changing, O Frog who is a prince?"

I stood up to my full frog height and said proudly, "Because I am a frog who is a frog. Like I was telling you, I'm just a plain frog. Anywhere you look, wherever you see a frog, it is really a frog. Same thing with dogs, birds, fish, etcetera. I cannot be other than what I truly am. You should accept someone for what he is, O Princess, and not for what you want him to be."

That was my big speech. It had the moral of the play. Miss Stemmish had insisted upon a moral.

I continued, "Do not be sad, O Princess. Find a prince who is really a prince and you will find happiness. I hope that my being a genuine frog won't spoil our friendship. Come and visit me anytime here. I will be glad to see you. Good-bye."

"Good-bye, O Frog, and thank you for being wiser than I."

I think that Maggie stuck her tongue out slightly as she said that line, but I'm not sure. Noah led her away to the palace.

I wasn't in the last scene. Ronald the Rock Thrower arrived at the palace. "I am prince of another country," he said, "and I was just passing by. I heard that there is an injured princess and so I came here to see her." Ronald really strutted across the stage. He was disgusting.

"O Prince, I am so happy to see you. I have been waiting for you by the pond. But you never showed up."

"I am here now and we will now live happily ever after," said Ronald the Rock Thrower.

"Yes, we will," said Maggie. "And we will visit the frog pond often. For wisdom is there."

"What an enchanting ending," said Miss Stemmish. "But I cringe at some of your language. I would adore changing just a few teeny tiny lines here and there."

"We're all memorized," said Ronald. He was afraid of losing his opening line "I am prince of another country." He was just crazy about that line, the show-off.

"Very well. That's all for today," said Miss Stemmish.

"Not yet," squeaked Maggie. She opened up a very large shopping bag that she had brought her ketchup in. "I've got a little treat for the cast. Some bread pudding."

I wanted to run. I wanted to run far and fast. But everybody would notice.

Maggie looked me in the eye even more closely than when she was hoping I'd turn into a prince. "My mother baked this, but she had some help from a *real* cook. You'll never guess who the cook was."

Maggie kept looking at me. She didn't know that I had gone back to my frog role. If I could convince myself for the next few minutes that I was really a frog, nothing except a frog-catcher could harm me.

But I wasn't a frog, and I was about to be exposed as a sissy cook. And I had somehow, somewhere missed the chance to get something on Maggie. If I had been smarter, luckier, faster, maybe I would have gotten something.

Henry said, "How many of you think the palace should be painted medium blue?"

Maggie said very slowly, "I'll tell all of you some-time who the cook was."

Why didn't she tell them then and there? Was there something good inside of Maggie Marmel-stein? Or did she see something good in me?

She passed around paper plates and plastic spoons.

She even gave me a plate and a spoon. "For you, Thaddeus Gideon Smith the Fifth," she said. "I wouldn't forget you."

"I won't forget you either," I said. "Just wait. You'll see."

The bread pudding was delicious. I thought I could taste the banana and jellies, which had been my contribution. But this couldn't have been the same bread pudding I had helped make. If it was, this bread pudding was not only unsanitary, it was senile.

When Henry and I were walking home, he said, "Well, Maggie almost spilled the beans—I mean the bread pudding—today. So what have you found out about *her*?"

"How good a friend are you?" I asked.

"The best," said Henry.

"Okay, then. A best friend is loyal even to a loser. A loser, that's me. I found out nothing."

"Nothing? You must have found out something after all this time."

"Oh, sure," I said. "I almost forgot. I found out that Maggie uses Heinz ketchup."

A Smart Mouse
Is Maggie Marmelstein

We were buying a gift for Miss Stemmish. To thank
her for directing our play. And for her bravery above
and beyond the call of duty? No. For being chicken
and letting us have our way. We were also buying it
because Miss Stemmish is a lovely lady. That's how
the principal once described her when he was in a
good mood. The class knew that Miss Stemmish is
too lovely for her own good, but somehow that made
her even lovelier.

We each contributed 25¢, so we had $6.75 to
spend. But who would pick out the gift? Miss
Stemmish was out of the classroom, so now was the
time to ask for volunteers. Guess who volunteered?
Maggie Marmelstein, of course. "Only if someone
will go along with me," said Maggie.

I have read plenty of adventure books where there
is a dangerous mission, and I can always figure out in

advance what people are destined to go on it, and what people are destined to stay behind. So just as I knew in advance who would get to go in the books, I knew that I, Thaddeus Gideon Smith the Fifth, would be going on this real-life mission.

Then my good friend Henry spoke up. "I think the princess and the frog should go together."

Sometimes Henry is too helpful. Good friends are supposed to be tuned in to each other at all times, whether they are talking or silent. But sometimes Henry appeared to be tuned in to a bunch of static instead of me. He should have known that I did not want to go with Maggie.

Henry looked at me and sort of twisted his mouth. It was his way of telling me something he couldn't tell me.

Of course! A terrific chance for GSOMMM. I was the one who was tuned in to static.

"I accept and look forward to the challenge," I said. That was a line from one of my books, which was said by someone who never came back from his mission.

Henry was eager. "Miss Stemmish is rehearsing just the palace people today, so you and Maggie can go right after school."

Maggie hadn't said a word. Henry and I had been too enthusiastic, and Maggie seemed suspicious. But she said that she would go.

After school Maggie and I went to Borack's Department Store. We had a list of possible presents that the kids had suggested. A scarf, perfume, monogrammed stationery, if we could find some already equipped with an S, and handkerchiefs.

First we stopped at a perfume counter. Maggie opened bottles and sniffed. She sniffed with real style.

The saleslady said, "It smells different on each person."

"We didn't bring the person along," said Maggie. Maggie walked away and I followed. "Let's try the scarves and handkerchiefs," she said. At the scarves counter Maggie draped a scarf around her neck. "That looks good on you," I said. "But it won't look so great on Miss Stemmish."

Why did I say that? Because it was true. Maggie gave me an odd look and she took off the scarf. She examined the handkerchiefs at the next counter. There were some nice ones with different colored borders.

"We could get a different color for each day of

the week," I said. "Miss Stemmish could use handy reminders like that, if she could get used to them."

"My bread comes with a different colored plastic tie around the wrapper for each day of the week," said Maggie.

Bread! Bread snuggled into Hackensack, New Jersey, bread wrappers, bread snuggled into bread pudding. Bread—the Battle Cry!

Maggie studied the handkerchiefs. She was not reacting to her own battle cry. She was cool. The worst kind of enemy is a cool enemy. Dumb and cool is worse than smart and hot, if you can choose a combination. I finally admitted to myself that Maggie wasn't dumb either. A smart, cool mouse is Maggie Marmelstein.

"Let's look around some more," she said.

We walked up and down aisles. Maggie didn't say anything that couldn't safely be printed on the front page of a newspaper.

Even though she was out shopping with a rat and a cook, and I was out shopping with a mouse, we were polite to each other. She was too suspicious to be nasty to me, and I was too watchful to be nasty to her. She kept sizing me up like I was merchandise on sale at Borack's Department Store, and I was doing the same to her. I had a goal, and she had a goal of finding out my goal.

I tried hard. "Want to get Miss Stemmish a diary?" I asked. "Do you keep a diary?"

"No to both questions," said Maggie.

"Don't you do anything you'd like to keep private? You know, secret things?"

"Sure," said Maggie. "I like to take baths in private. Don't you?"

"Sure."

"And when I do my homework I like to be alone."

"Me, too."

Yep, Maggie was cool.

We stopped at a table that had tiny glasses and vases and figures on it. "Eeeee," squeaked Maggie. I saw what she saw. A frog about three inches high with a hole in his back and some flowers stuck in the hole. A little sticker was stuck to him. On it was printed $4.95.

"We'll take him," said Maggie without asking me.

"Hey, it's up to me, too," I said.

"Well?" she said.

"We'll take him."

She smiled as if she had scored. I lost more than I gained insisting on my rights.

We bought a card and some extra flowers for the frog's back with the money we had left over. "I'm going to wrap it myself," said Maggie. "I've got some 'Congratulations' paper at home."

We walked home to our apartment house. At her door, Maggie said, "Thanks for your help. If you want to know anything else, I keep all my secrets in a tunnel dug under the floor of my room and I keep the entrance to the tunnel locked with a giant padlock, and the key to the padlock is hidden under a rock in San Francisco Bay."

Then she went into her apartment. She had caught on to what I was up to. Me and my stupid questions. I had something in common with the frog we bought, but my hole was in my head, and it didn't have any flowers sticking out of it.

"Dear Cary Grant"

It was Thursday, and I was at the door of the Marmelstein apartment again. Apartment 2B was where my troubles started, and I was afraid I would get sucked into more trouble this time. But I knew that Maggie would be at school rehearsing for at least another hour. And besides, Henry had said this might be a good place for GSOMMM.

I rang the bell. Mrs. Marmelstein answered right away. "I've been expecting you, O Frog," she said, and she smiled. She was sort of draped in material that had pins stuck in it. She reminded me of an enormous pincushion. I was sorry that she did, but she did. The cooking part of her was off duty, I thought, because I couldn't smell any food.

"Come on in," she said, "and see what a handsome frog you're going to be. Just wait till you see your material."

She led me into the living room. Material was draped over the sofa and the chairs and some of the floor. She held up something green and shiny. "Here you are. Comfortable and permanent-press, too. Maggie says you hop around in your pond, but you'll look neat, I guarantee it. Do you like it? You shouldn't wear anything you don't like."

"So far so good," I said.

"Good," said Mrs. Marmelstein. "So now we hang and fit."

Mrs. Marmelstein wrapped the shiny green material around me, and pinned it in a few places. Then she measured me in different directions and made some notes. "Do frogs have tails?" she asked. "I'm not up on my frogs."

"I'm not either," I said. "But it would be great with me if they don't."

"Here, let's look up frogs in Maggie's reference book," said Mrs. Marmelstein.

She walked into Maggie's bedroom and I decided to follow. I thought it was a bedroom because there was a bed in it, but if someone had said it was a photo gallery, I might have believed him. All over the walls, north to south and east to west, were pictures of actors cut from newspapers and magazines. I knew they were actors because actors do not take the same kind of picture as other people. Other people hardly ever take a picture swinging from a treetop or wearing a uniform of the Foreign Legion or running away from Frankenstein.

"You're admiring my Maggie's pictures," said Mrs. Marmelstein.

"I guess the landlord never has to paint this room," I said. "Where did Maggie get all these pictures?"

"She cut up my old movie magazines," said Mrs. Marmelstein. "And she arranged the pictures on the wall all by herself. She's had this arranging talent since she was a baby."

"Is this a hobby or something?" I asked. "How come she put up the pictures?"

"Oh, my Maggie loves acting and actors," said Mrs. Marmelstein.

"How much does she love them?" I asked.

"How much? Oh, much! She even writes letters to them," said Mrs. Marmelstein.

"Really? Who does she write to?"

"Well, let me see. This week alone she wrote to Rock Hudson, John Wayne, Henry Fonda, Spencer

Tracy, Cary Grant, and Clark Gable, to mention a few."

"Aren't some of them dead?" I asked.

"Maggie doesn't want to know who's dead and who's alive," said Mrs. Marmelstein. "She writes to them all and hopes for the best. She mails out a few at a time so that there's always hope of hearing from somebody, if not tomorrow, maybe the next day. She had trouble composing the first letter so she sends everybody the same kind."

Mrs. Marmelstein took a book from a bookcase. "Well, back to the frog business," she said. "There's one page that has pictures of a real variety of frogs. Here. Do you want to be a pickerel frog, a bullfrog, or a common green frog? I've already got material for a green frog, so it would be nice if that's what you want to be."

"That's exactly it, on the button. A common green frog," I said.

"Settled," said Mrs. Marmelstein. "And unless he's sitting on it, he doesn't have a tail." She closed the book. "I'll make the costume so that it will fit right over your regular clothes," she said. "So you won't feel you're only one layer away from your underwear. And I'll zipper you from head to toe.

Then it will be easy to step in and out. Next time you come over, I'll have it ready to try on. Now, maybe you're hungry, being draped over and pinned on. I'm out of that bread pudding, but I've got chocolate cookies and peach pie."

"I'll take the peach pie, please," I said. "Mind if I look over this book while you're getting ready in the kitchen?"

"Sure, look," said Mrs. Marmelstein. "It's very educational. But we settled on the common green frog. Don't change your mind now."

"Never," I said.

Mrs. Marmelstein went into the kitchen, thinking she had left behind her a serious student of frogs. But I had no intention of looking at the book. Now I knew that Maggie wrote to all kinds of actors. Maybe this was the big break I'd been hoping for. I was wondering what the letters said. Somewhere in this room there might be a letter. Evidence!

I walked around the room, peeking, peering, hoping. Nothing interesting. Nothing. Suddenly I remembered Maggie's remark about her secret tunnel. Of course she was just being a wise guy, but maybe she wasn't wise enough. There is sometimes a tiny bit of truth hidden in a phony story, like a hole in a piece of cheese. I stared at the floor. And I thought. Then I bent down and looked at the floor under Maggie's bed. There were three large boxes under the bed. I pulled one out. It had MAGGIE MARMELSTEIN, PRIVATE printed across the top. Oh, wonderful hole in the cheese!

Boxes marked PRIVATE can be considered invitations when a person is hunting for evidence. So I opened the box. It contained just what I was looking for. Letters. The other boxes probably contained more of just what I was looking for. But I had to work fast, so I concentrated on box number one. I unfolded one of the letters. I read it.

DEAR CARY GRANT,
I LOVE TO WATCH YOU ON TELEVISION AND MY MOTHER LOVES TO WATCH YOU AND MY FATHER SOMETIMES LOVES TO WATCH YOU. COULD YOU PLEASE SEND ME A PICTURE OF YOURSELF SO I COULD WATCH YOU ALL THE TIME? I AM SENDING YOU TEN CENTS IN CASE IT COSTS MONEY. PLEASE KEEP THIS LETTER PRIVATE BECAUSE I DON'T WANT ANYBODY TO KNOW ABOUT IT EXCEPT YOU

AND ME AND MAYBE MY MOTHER. PLEASE
WRITE ON THE PICTURE TO MY FRIEND
MAGGIE MARMELSTEIN FROM HER FRIEND
CARY GRANT.
  LOVE,
  YOUR FRIEND MAGGIE MARMELSTEIN

"Ready, my common green frog," called Mrs. Marmelstein.

"Your common green frog is coming," I called back. I stuffed the Cary Grant letter into my pocket, closed the box and shoved it under the bed.

Mrs. Marmelstein and I sat at her kitchen table eating peach pie and drinking milk. The nicer she was to me, the worse I felt. But I was thinking that maybe someday, when I grew up and became rich, I'd go out and buy her a mink coat or a diamond bracelet and send it to her anonymously to make up for taking advantage of her. On second thought, maybe I'd get her a new mixing spoon, solid gold, but usable.

"Maggie will be coming home soon," she said. "I'm glad that she got to be your princess and you got to be her frog. That's nice." Mrs. Marmelstein smiled.

Maybe I'd send her two solid gold spoons.

"I have to go do my homework now," I said. "Thanks for the pie and the costume—and everything."

"My pleasure," she said. "I'll see you in a few days. I'll be sewing you over the weekend and it should be ready for you to try on by Monday."

I called Henry the minute I got back to my apartment. "Come over quick. It's about GSOMMM. I'll give you a hint. I've got SOMMM."

Henry established new speed records in running over to my apartment. I handed him the Cary Grant letter. Henry established new speed records in reading. "This is absolutely nutty," he said. "A love letter to Cary Grant."

"And," I said, "she wrote the same letter to John Wayne, Henry Fonda, Rock Hudson, to loads and loads of guys."

"Hey, aren't some of them old enough to be her grandfather?" asked Henry.

"Not on The Late Show, they're not," I said. "Whatever age they were when the movie was made, that's where they stay. Forever. Some day Maggie's going to be older than Cary Grant."

"All I've got to say is congratulations, pal. This is

definitely the big news you've been hopping for. Hopping, get it?"

Then Henry called me a genius. That was better than I deserved. Lucky and sneaky was what I deserved.

After Henry left, I read the letter over and over again. This was Maggie's private letter that wouldn't be private much longer, when everybody found out that she wrote love letters. And I had the actual evidence. She really didn't have any evidence on me, like say a picture of me in the apron stirring the pudding.

I, Thaddeus Gideon Smith the Fifth, was at last a winner.

We Go to
Miss Stemmish's House

It was hard not to use the evidence immediately, but Maggie believed in springing news at exactly the right time, and for once I agreed with Maggie. My exactly right time would be right after the play, while the cast was still around. I could have made a deal with Maggie. If she wouldn't tell about cook, I wouldn't tell about Cary. But Cary had it all over cook. It would have been like trading a million dollars for a fifty-cent piece.

I wondered if Maggie or her mother had noticed that Cary Grant was missing. I didn't think so.

I went for my second frog-suit fitting the day before dress rehearsal. I picked that day because Maggie was at school rehearsing again and I wasn't needed.

"I was beginning to think you changed your mind," said Mrs. Marmelstein. "I was telling my friends I was stood up by a frog. Well, here's your costume. Step right into it."

Mrs. Marmelstein took a few last-minute stitches after I tried on the costume. It was very comfortable and very shiny. I gazed at myself in the mirror. I couldn't believe that the strange creature I saw had me inside him. Mrs. Marmelstein had done a terrific job, and I told her so.

"Mostly I did it while I watched *The Wizard of Oz*," she said. "It put me in the mood."

I didn't stay for the cookies she offered me. All I could think of was Cary Grant and getting out of the apartment as fast as possible.

After dress rehearsal the next day, we all changed back to our civilian clothes. We were going over to Miss Stemmish's house for the cast party and to give her the present. Usually a cast party takes place after the play is over, but Miss Stemmish was probably afraid there wouldn't be anything to celebrate by then. However, since Miss Stemmish would promise anything to promote peace and happiness, she had also promised us another party after the play.

Miss Stemmish's house is only a few blocks from school, so all of us walked over together. Miss Stemmish led the way, and appointed Noah to guard the rear. Noah took his job seriously, which meant he watched Ronald all the way. He always does that anyway, ready to duck at the slightest movement of Ronald's hand toward his pocket, where a supply of rocks might be available. By the time we got to Miss Stemmish's house, it had been a four-duck walk for Noah.

As we marched up the front walk, I suddenly wondered what any of us were doing here, including Miss Stemmish. I never imagined her having a house or an apartment or, in fact, anything besides a school in her life. In my mind, Miss Stemmish existed for the one and only purpose of showing up at her English classes each day.

And now a house! And parents! Miss Stemmish lived with her mother and father. Her father greeted us at the door. He told us right away that he was 86 years old. "Everybody always buzzes around my head, trying to figure out my age," he said. "So I may as well save them the trouble. My wife won't tell her age, but she'll never see 87 again, I'll tell you that much."

Mrs. Stemmish was in the kitchen working over a big punch bowl. She and her husband looked like twins, thin with white hair and crinkly faces. And they were lively. I was relieved to see that they were having such a healthy old age. It was a hopeful sign for a long life for Miss Stemmish, who always seemed about to collapse.

We all sat in the huge living room, some of us on chairs, most of us on the floor. Everybody was using their party personality. Henry told some frog jokes he had been collecting, and everybody laughed, even at the bad ones. One of the kids started to sing, and the whole group joined in. And surprise! Old Mr. Stemmish had the kind of strong voice that only needed a handlebar moustache, three other guys, and maybe a barber pole to be complete.

Miss Stemmish and Mrs. Stemmish passed around punch, cake, and popcorn. I noticed how much Miss Stemmish looked like her parents, except that wherever they were, she hadn't gotten there yet. There was something that seemed strange about the three of them living in this house, but I had exactly the same arrangement with my parents—two parents and one child under the same roof—and it was a pretty popular setup among my friends, too.

After we ate, Miss Stemmish showed us around the house. It was a big house and probably old enough for George Washington to have slept in if he had ever been in the neighborhood. Almost all of the walls were covered with paintings, beautiful paintings, and each one was signed C. Stemmish. Miss Stemmish was an artist!

Miss Stemmish said, "My *heart* is in art, but my degree is in English."

That explained a lot of things. Miss Stemmish was most likely more comfortable with pictures than with words. A fish out of water was Miss Stemmish. Henry would say that's why she flounders so.

"I'm taking some art courses this summer," said Miss Stemmish, "and I hope to become an art teacher. I should have done it years ago. Years and years and years ago."

Miss Stemmish fluttered about like a surprised feather that had suddenly been evicted from a pillow. She looked embarrassed. She had shown us her house and her hopes, and she had only meant to show us her house.

Maggie squeaked up, "Your paintings are pretty."

I had forgotten about Maggie in The World of Miss Stemmish. Was it possible?

Maggie took a package from the shopping bag that had recently been the carrier of ketchup and bread pudding. The package looked clean and colorful. It contained the flower-growing frog. Our class was anxious to present the gift to Miss Stemmish so that she could enjoy it before the play. Naturally Maggie was the presenter. "For you, from us," she squeaked. "With thanks."

Miss Stemmish said, "You shouldn't have," and unwrapped the package. The flowers in the frog's back were only slightly bent. "Oh, he is exquisite," gasped Miss Stemmish. She held him up. "I will always treasure this frog."

Maggie smiled at me. A friendly, we-did-a-good-job smile.

There are ladies' and gentlemen's rules for an occasion like this, and we observed them. Between Maggie and me there was a truce. I smiled back. At this moment, at this time and place, I meant it.

"So Nervous
You Could Croak."

At last it was the night of the play. My parents, Mr. and Mrs. Stemmish, and Mr. and Mrs. Marmelstein were in the front row. Mrs. Marmelstein was overlapping Mr. Marmelstein who is very thin. She was leaning on the armrest between them, and Mr. Marmelstein had the lost, squashed look of someone who knew he would never get to use it. In the game of Who Gets the Armrest, Mr. Marmelstein has probably been a loser all his married life.

The principal was also in the front row. I was thinking that he and Maggie had something in common. They were in for the biggest surprises of the evening.

Henry helped me with my costume. "You look snazzy," he said as he zipped me up. "Don't be nervous just because you've got a leading role and everyone is counting on you and will be watching you."

I wanted to say, "Henry, while you're at it, zipper your lip, too." But I said, "Thanks for zipping me up."

Our class was backstage, waiting. Somebody took our picture in our costumes. Then we took a picture with Miss Stemmish who was dressed in a bunch of flowers and something purple to the floor.

It made me jittery to wait. Henry said, "You're so nervous you could croak." He laughed. He could afford to laugh. He had only a few lines to remember.

"I wish I had stayed as one of the palace people," I said. "I'm sorry I got into this frog business."

"Yuh, but look what you've accomplished," he said. "Remember Cary Grant."

Somehow, when Henry said that, it made me feel more nervous.

It was time to go on. I took my place on the green rug. It was loaded with so many ketchup stains that the Salvation Army would probably turn it down now. The curtain went up. Everybody applauded. Maggie came walking across the stage. More applause. She walked up to the rug and sat down next to it. She said, "Hello, Frog. Are you new here? I never noticed you in the pond before."

I said, "Hello, Princess. This is my first day in the pond."

Everything was just about perfect. Maggie knew her lines and I knew mine. And the rest of the cast came on okay, too. There was a slip now and then, but nothing big.

In the scenes where the princess was back at the palace, and all I had to do was sit on the rug, I had a chance to look around. Miss Stemmish was beaming from the wings, but once in a while she flinched as if someone had hit her. I noticed that the principal was kind of slouching.

It was time for the bleeding scene. It went off very well until Doc Noah said, "I will bind up your wound. And here are two aspirin."

I heard a "No!" from the direction of Miss Stemmish. At this point Noah should have offered the aspirin to her. I didn't think the audience heard the No. Noah went on with his lines, "And you will be all right. This frog here has saved your life."

"That's it!" cried Maggie. "That is just how a frog could lift the evil spell. I will kiss you, O Frog, and you will become a prince."

Maggie gave me a longer kiss than she had in rehearsals. It felt like she was making a slight dent in my face, which I was sure would come out almost immediately. Anyway, this time I didn't feel like scratching the place.

Then she said, "Why aren't you changing, O Frog who is a prince?"

I stood up to my full frog height. It was time for my big speech about how I really am a frog now and forever. I said, "Because I am a frog who is a . . ." I stopped. As I stood up, my head-to-toe zipper had started to unzip, and slowly I was unzipping from head to toe. As I was unzipping, I grabbed the suit and held it up around my waist. The audience gasped. I would gladly have changed places with any person in the world. Especially Henry. But right then and there I promised myself that I would still be Henry's friend, and that I would even be extra kind to him, because anyone who can't fasten a zipper at his age is desperately in need of help and friendship.

I looked at Miss Stemmish. Since she was the director, maybe she would signal me what to do. She put her hands over her face. I put my hands over my face.

My shiny green frog suit slithered to my feet.

Now We Will Live
Happily Ever After

Maggie and I stood there like a dumbstruck princess and a dumbstruck ex-frog in dungarees and polo shirt. About a thousand years went by, I'd say, and we just stood there.

Then Maggie clasped her ketchup-covered hands. "My prince!" she exclaimed. "Even in your ragged clothes I can tell you are my prince. Hurry let us go to the palace and tell my mother and father. Hurry."

I was glad to leave the rug. I couldn't think of anything else to do there. I stepped out of the bunch of frog suit at my feet. Then Maggie walked toward the palace and sort of dragged me along. Noah followed with his big bag. Maggie and I went up to the king and queen.

"I have found my prince," Maggie said, "and now we will live happily ever after."

The king and queen looked confused. Maggie

nudged Queen Ellen. Ellen opened her mouth, and in a louder voice than I had ever heard her use, she said, "Oh my daughter, I am so happy for you!"

Ellen had actually done some original thinking. And it was good original thinking. Maggie said to her, "And I am happy for you."

I could see Ronald the Rock Thrower out in the wings waiting to come on. Suddenly he strutted out. "I am prince of another country," he boomed. Noah strutted after him.

"Your country just went out of business," Noah boomed back, and he hit Ronald over the head with his physician's bag. I knew he had been wanting to do that for a long time. Now he had all these witnesses to his daring act.

"Curtain!" yelled Miss Stemmish. As the curtain came down, Maggie turned toward the audience and smiled a happily-ever-after smile, so I did, too.

The applause we got was fantastic. I'll never know why. And we got several curtain calls. Maggie and I were supposed to be in front, and the rest of the cast in back, but Noah came up and shared the front with us. I think he was afraid to be in back with Ronald. Noah was very pleased with himself. Maybe he couldn't get rid of the sissy label in one swoop,

but at least he knew he was on the way.

After the last curtain call, Miss Stemmish shook all our hands, including Ronald's and Noah's. She was the commander-in-chief congratulating the troops after the battle, although she hadn't the foggiest idea whether they had won or lost.

During the curtain calls, I noticed that the principal wasn't clapping. He was busy writing something. It was a note to our class, which was delivered a few minutes later by another teacher. The teacher read it out loud. "Congratulations! You have infused an old fairy tale with a vitality and spirit that is both commendable and entertaining."

Miss Stemmish tried hard not to look astonished. She started to hum. We were all glad for her, because her victories were few and far between. She shook Maggie's hand a few more times. "You are a bright, bright girl," she said.

Maggie smiled. This was her big moment. All the kids had heard what Miss Stemmish said. "Thank you," squeaked Maggie.

This could be my big moment, too. I put my hand inside my dungaree pocket. The letter was there. I pulled it out.

Good-bye, Cary,
Good-bye, Cook

Maggie wasn't paying any attention.

I said to her, "I have a public announcement to make." Then I waved the letter in front of her face, slowly enough for her to recognize it, then faster so she couldn't grab it. She looked absolutely shocked. After she stopped looking shocked, I found out that she had an even meaner look than she had given me in the past. And finally, she only looked sad.

She had gone from happy to shocked to mean to sad in about one minute. Suddenly Maggie was a lost mouse. And she didn't say anything. And I didn't say anything. Henry came up and nudged me. He was my cheerleader for the Cary Grant event. But I didn't want a cheerleader, because I didn't want to go through with it. After all, for almost two weeks Maggie'd been my princess and I'd been her frog. And she wasn't all bad. If it weren't for Maggie,

I could have been standing on that stage forever, unzipped and unfrogged. And she was able to be a real friend to Ellen. And to Noah too. Maybe because they needed a friend. And she thought I didn't. But even though I have Henry, I can always use extras. Actually, Maggie wasn't bad at all, if you didn't expect her to be a lot better. Like the frog said, if you expect a frog to be a frog, fine. But if you expect a prince, forget it.

I handed her the letter. "This belongs to you," I said.

"Thanks," she said. She took the letter, but she didn't go away. She was thinking things over. What was she thinking? On the one hand, I took her letter. On the other hand, I didn't use it. On the one hand, I told her she squeaked like a mouse. On the other hand, I came to her rescue in class afterward. She was weighing me on the scales of justice. While she was at it, I hoped she was weighing herself, too.

Slowly she broke out in a friendly smile. Then she said in her best princess voice, "Even in your ragged clothes I can tell you are my prince."

This time Maggie wasn't acting. I even thought she was going to kiss me again. I hoped not.

She didn't. She stuck the letter in one of her

princess pockets and walked away, still smiling. She had just played a genuine happy-ending scene. I was happy too. Good-bye, Cary, good-bye, cook.

Henry had been watching and listening, silently, which was an amazing accomplishment for Henry. After Maggie walked away, he said, "Why didn't you do it?"

"Henry," I said, "you've got more important things to worry about. Like the new game I'm inventing for you called Zipper-Up."

"How do you mean that, pal? Look, about the zipper. I'm sure I fastened it."

"It's okay, Henry. You know Shakespeare said, 'All's well that ends well'."

"I'm for that," said Henry.

Miss Stemmish called, "Class, class, we will now go to the gym for our party."

"I'm for that, too," said Henry.

Everybody started to leave for the gym, but I was stopped just as I was about to step down from the stage. I was stopped by Mrs. Marmelstein. "My poor common green frog. Betrayed by a zipper. But you were marvelous." Mrs. Marmelstein put her arm around me. "I came to inspect the zipper."

Henry said, "See you later, pal."

The frog suit was on a chair where I had put it. Mrs. Marmelstein picked it up and started zippering. Up, fasten. Down, up, fasten. Down, up, fasten. Down, up, fasten.

"It works to perfection," she said. "Let's try a few more times to be positively positive."

I was feeling bad again about Mrs. Marmelstein. I had just unloaded Cary Grant, and with him, my guilty conscience about being a sneak. But if I told Mrs. Marmelstein that her zipper was perfect, I would reveal that my friend Henry was perfectly dumb at zippering.

Mrs. Marmelstein saved the day. "Fate unzipped you," she said finally.

I was free again. But wait! Mrs. Marmelstein was taking something out of her pocketbook. "For you, my common green frog," she said.

It was her recipe for bread pudding.

"I wrote it down for you," she said. "I cook by ear, but a beginner like you should cook by print. I knew you were too busy with the play, so I waited. So now, cook and enjoy."

Mrs. Marmelstein closed her pocketbook with a loud snap. The recipe cannot return, the entrance is closed, was the song of the snap. "And now I'm running," said Mrs. Marmelstein. "I'm helping out at the party. Come, you'll be late."

"I'll be along soon," I said. I watched her leave the auditorium.

Fortunately no one had heard our conversation. The stage was now deserted except for me. I stood there alone with Mrs. Marmelstein's handwritten recipe and I didn't know what to do with it. I couldn't bring myself to throw it away and I couldn't bring myself to keep it.

BREAD PUDDING

First put on old clothes or an apron.

INGREDIENTS

any stale dark bread you have around
any stale white bread ditto
milk (Look under instructions for how much.)
1 spoon brown sugar (the size of my spoon)
1 spoon white sugar (ditto)
a handful of nuts
ditto cut-up dates
double ditto raisins (I like raisins. Make it one hand-
    ful if you don't like them much.)

3 eggs

maybe ½ cup flour or matzoh meal

1 spoon molasses (the size of my spoon)

apricot jelly (You know how much.)

grape jelly (ditto)

a little applesauce if you have some, don't buy it special

any bananas lying around

½ stick of melted butter

1 drop of vanilla

baking soda (¼ the size of my spoon)

1 tiny glass of red wine (if your mother lets you)

some cinnamon (Figure out how much by ear, it's good practice.)

INSTRUCTIONS

Break up the bread and soak pieces in enough milk to soften the bread. Mix bread with all the other ingredients except the eggs and the flour or matzoh meal. Mix them up in any order. You don't have to be fussy. Keep tasting as you go along. Remember you can always add, but you can't subtract once you've added. After it's all mixed up, if it's thin looking, add some flour or matzoh meal until it gets thick looking. Now take your three eggs and separate the yolks and the whites. Maybe have your mother do this and you watch. Mix up the yolks with the rest of the mix. Beat the whites with an eggbeater until stiff (the whites). Then fold them into the mix, but gently—no enthusiasm please. Now grease any shape pan that looks big enough to hold everything, and pour everything into it. Sprinkle some more cinnamon on top. Remember you already sprinkled some inside. Bake it at 350 degrees for three quarters of an hour, maybe a little more, maybe a little less. Don't go out to play and forget about it. Wear big mitts to take it out of the oven (kitchen mitts, not Mickey Mantle mitts). Serve it hot with milk poured over it or cold. Bring some for me to sample.

Well, that's the recipe. If you like it, don't tell me. Tell Mrs. Marmelstein. Apartment 2B.

HARPER TROPHY BOOKS
you will enjoy reading

HARPER & ROW, PUBLISHERS, INC.
10 East 53rd Street, New York, New York 10022